Dying to Cook

Asheville Meadows Cozy Mysteries

Book Five

By

Patti Benning

.

Author's Note: On the next page, you'll find out how to access all of my books easily, as well as locate books by best-selling author, Summer Prescott. I'd love to hear your thoughts on my books, the storylines, and anything else that you'd like to comment on – reader feedback is very important to me. Please see the following page for my publisher's contact information. If you'd like to be on her list of "folks to contact" with updates, release and sales notifications, etc...just shoot her an email and let her know. Thanks for reading!

Also…

…if you're looking for more great reads, from me and Summer, check out the Summer Prescott Publishing Book Catalog:

http://summerprescottbooks.com/book-catalog/ for some truly delicious stories.

Contact Info for Summer Prescott Publishing:

Twitter: @summerprescott1

Blog and Book Catalog:
http://summerprescottbooks.com

Email: summer.prescott.cozies@gmail.com

And…look up The Summer Prescott Fan Page and Summer Prescott Publishing Page on Facebook – let's be friends!

To sign up for our fun and exciting newsletter, which will give you opportunities to win prizes and swag, enter contests, and be the first to know about New Releases, click here:
https://forms.aweber.com/form/02/1682036602.htm

TABLE OF CONTENTS

DYING TO COOK

Asheville Meadows Cozy Mysteries

Book Five

CHAPTER ONE

Autumn Roth put her purse down in the staff room and checked the noticeboard. Sometimes, the other chef who worked at Asheville Meadows left her a note if they had run out of an ingredient unexpectedly, or if something interesting had happened during one of the meals, but there wasn't anything for her today. She glanced at Nicholas Holt's office but turned away when she heard the murmur of his voice through the door. Nick Holt was the director of Asheville Meadows... and also, her boyfriend. Work kept him busy for large portions of the day, but she knew that he would stop by the kitchen later to say hi to her. Seeing him at work daily was one of the many benefits of working at the nursing home, though she still wasn't completely comfortable with the fact that she was dating the boss.

She had a few minutes before she had to get started on lunch, so she decided to make a detour on the way to the kitchen to her aunt and uncle's room. Her Aunt Lucinda had suffered a stroke a couple of years beforehand, and though she had made slow progress, she was still unable to speak, walk, or care for herself. Her Uncle Albert was clearheaded and capable of getting around just fine, even though he had lost part of his leg when he fought in a war in his youth, but he had opted to move into the nursing home with his wife rather than stay at their old home alone.

"Autumn," her uncle said in surprise when he opened the door to see her standing in the hall. "We were just talking about you. Come on in. I take it you have to get cooking soon?"

"Yes," Autumn said as she sidled into the room. "We're having cauliflower soup, fruit salad, and homemade bread for lunch today."

"That sounds good," her uncle said. "I'm half-starved already. Of course, I'd find room for one of your meals even if I was stuffed to the gills. Anyway, I'm sure you remember Westley. He was over here for a cup of coffee while we watched a rerun of the game from last weekend."

Autumn turned and realized that her aunt and uncle weren't the only people in the apartment. There was a third person; an elderly man with a shock of white hair and a richly styled wooden cane. Westley Phillips, the famous mystery writer.

"It's nice to see you again," she said, nodding to the other man. "You haven't been at any meals this week, have you?"

"I had a bout of pneumonia," he said. "They packed me off to the hospital just to be safe. I'm back now, and all better." He covered up a cough, then chuckled. "Well, for the most part."

"That's good, I'm glad you're back," Autumn said. She walked across the room and crouched down to give her Aunt Lucy a hug.

"Your aunt has been making progress with her physical therapy," Uncle Al said from behind her. "Show her, Lucy."

Autumn watched in thrilled surprise as her aunt raised her bad hand and formed a shaky, weak fist.

"That's amazing," she breathed. "I knew you could do it. You must be so happy that you're still making progress. In no time at all, you'll be up and walking around."

Aunt Lucy just gave her a lopsided smile, then patted her hand. Autumn wondered if her aunt still hoped to regain full use of her faculties, or if she had resigned herself to living with limited mobility for the rest of her life. She wanted to think that her aunt still had hope. Autumn firmly believed that hope was important in life, even if the thing that you were hoping for seemed far out of reach.

"Would you like some coffee, or maybe a cup of tea?" her uncle asked.

"Thanks, but I can only stay for a couple of minutes. I'll just grab some coffee from the machine in the kitchen once I get to work."

"My coffee is better, but suit yourself," he said. "So, is there anything new with you? How's that little dog of yours doing?"

"Frankie is doing well," Autumn said. "I'll bring her to visit sometime. And no, there's nothing new with me. Just the same old, same old. Not that I'm complaining; I love working here, and I'm glad life has finally calmed down a bit. I think I might need to find a hobby or something, though."

A few minutes later, Autumn excused herself. It was time to get started on lunch. She promised her aunt and uncle that she would see them during the meal, took her leave of Westley Phillips, then stepped out of the room. In the months that she had worked at Asheville Meadows, she had come to know the place like the back of her hand. It was late morning, and residents were on their way to and from physical therapy, walks in the garden, and visits with relatives. Of the thirty residents there, about twenty could make their way through the halls on their own. The other ten required assistance to go anywhere and took up much of the staff's time. She was grateful that her aunt had her uncle to help her out. While the staff at Asheville Meadows did their jobs well and cared about the residents, there was nothing like having family to help you when you needed it.

When she walked into the kitchen, she found Nick waiting for her. He was leaning on the counter, scrolling through his phone, but looked up when she came in.

"I saw your purse in the office," he said. "I must have been on the phone when you came in. I just wanted to say hi."

"Hi," she said, smiling and feeling a hint of the butterflies that she had felt in her stomach every day since they had started going out. She had never liked anyone that she had dated as much as she liked Nick and hoped that she never lost that feeling.

"We'll be having a few guests for lunch today," he said. "You shouldn't need to make too much extra food, but make sure that there is enough for at least a few more servings than usual."

"I will," she promised. "How are you? I missed you yesterday."

"Busy," he said, running a hand down his face. "That call was from a local contractor who wanted to put a bid in on the addition."

Autumn had been reaching for the refrigerator's handle but paused. "A contractor?"

"Yes." His face split into a wide grin. "I didn't want to tell you until the board cleared it, but someone anonymously donated a large sum of money so we could add an extra wing to the building. The board already had a set of plans drawn up, so as soon as we find a contractor to take the job, construction will begin."

"Oh, Nick, that's wonderful!" Autumn threw her arms around him, and he chuckled as he returned the hug.

"I'm pretty excited myself," he said. "It will be wonderful to expand this place. The new wing will be for the residents that are more able to care for themselves. It will also allow dogs, as long as they are well behaved, since many residents have mentioned missing their pets, and we are going to add a small courtyard to it as well. I think this will be wonderful for everyone. The residents that need more constant care will stay in this part of the building, where they are closer to the dining room and the activity rooms. It's going to make things a lot easier for everyone and will also enable us to take in more residents."

"I can't wait to see it when it's done," Autumn said.

"Unfortunately, that probably won't be for a while. It's going to be a mess around here while the construction is happening. It will be worth it in the long run, though. I should let you get to work, shouldn't I? I'll stop by later today, around dinner time, and we can talk about our plans for this weekend. How would you feel about going hiking?"

"As long as the weather is as nice as it is today, I would be thrilled to go," she said. "I'll see you tonight."

He gave her a quick, chaste peck on the cheek, then left the room. Autumn smiled as she watched him go. Things just kept getting better and better. She couldn't have been happier for her boyfriend; he had wanted to expand the nursing home for a long time, and it was finally happening.

"Here you go, Uncle Al," she said, setting the bowl of cauliflower soup in front of him an hour later. "You might want to salt it yourself."

"I know, I know," he said. "I'm used to the low-sodium you have to serve here. I know my way around the saltshaker by now."

Autumn smiled, patted her aunt, who had already been served, on the arm, then turned to head back to the kitchen and grab the next set of bowls. She often helped with serving, since the nursing home was perpetually short staffed. She didn't mind; it gave her a chance to get to know the residents, something that she couldn't do very well while she was stuck in the kitchen.

"Pardon me," someone called out. Autumn turned to see a strict looking middle-aged woman — not a resident, or a guest that Autumn recognized — wave her over.

"How can I help you?" Autumn asked as she neared the table.

"Are you the cook?"

"I am. My name's Autumn Roth."

"I am Audrey Blake," the woman said. "I'm visiting my father for the first time in a while, and I thought I noticed a difference in the food."

"Sheldon Blake," Autumn said, smiling at the nonverbal elderly man to the woman's right. "I'm glad you have company today. Let me know if the two of you want anything special. I think we have some pudding left over from yesterday in the fridge."

"Wait, don't go yet," Audrey said as Autumn turned to leave, her mind still on the meals she had to serve. "I wanted to ask you something."

"Sure," Autumn said. "What is it?"

"All of this... do you make it by yourself?" she gestured at the food in front of her.

"For the most part, I do. Sometimes one of the other staff members helps me. Almost everything is made from scratch, though. Occasionally we'll use a cake mix or a brownie mix, but that's about it."

"I have to say, it's just wonderful," the woman said. "I understand that you have certain limitations, due to the dietary restrictions of the people you're serving, but even so, this food is delicious. Have you ever considered working in a real restaurant?"

"I have," Autumn admitted. "It's been a dream of mine for a long time, in fact."

Audrey looked around, then lowered her voice. "Listen... I have an opening at my restaurant right now. I've been going around town and rounding up people I think might make promising chefs, but who don't have the training that's usually required to work in a top-of-the-line restaurant. I want to give someone with hidden talent a chance that they might not have otherwise. Would you be interested in the position? Now, to be clear, you would still have to go through an interview process that includes working in the kitchen for a morning and proving that you can handle both the stress and the technical aspects of making a meal well under pressure, but it would be you and just a few other people trying out for the position. The pay would start off midrange, but it's probably better than what you make here."

Autumn hesitated, knowing that her mouth was hanging open in surprise. "I – I'm not sure. I love working here –"

"Oh, I know you do," the woman said. "I saw you talking to that older couple over there. It's obvious that you care about the residents quite a bit. We might even be able to work out something where you could still work here part-time, if you wanted. I just thought I would offer. I love encouraging people to use their talent, and I hate when I see it going to waste."

"I'll think about it," Autumn managed to say, still in shock at the offer. "Can I have your phone number?"

"Here's my business card, with my personal number on the back. Let me know your decision by Sunday, if you can. Like I said, I've got a few other people that will be trying out for the position as well. You did a wonderful job on the soup. I'd love to see what you can do in a *real* kitchen."

CHAPTER TWO

Autumn scrubbed intently at the countertop, watching as the coffee stain slowly faded away. It was Saturday morning, and in just under an hour her friends would be arriving for their first barbecue of the season. After the offer she had received from Audrey Blake, she hadn't been able to think of anything else. She needed to talk to the people closest to her in order to make up her mind. She and Nick could go hiking anytime, but this offer was something that would only happen once in her lifetime.

All her life, she had been enamored by the idea of being a professional chef. She had looked up Audrey Blake's restaurant and had known from the instant the website had loaded that it was exactly what she had always dreamed about. Now that the opportunity was right in front of her, however, she wasn't sure if she should take it. She loved working at Asheville Meadows. No, it wasn't the same as being a professional chef in a traditional kitchen, but it was deeply fulfilling in a way that no other job had been. It wasn't just the work; she loved being more involved with her aunt and uncle, and she enjoyed being around Nick, Emily, and all the other people that worked there. It wasn't just a job; it was a community. Even though she had only been working there for a few months, she already felt more at home there than she had at the grocery store, where she had worked for over five years.

"What should I do, Frankie?" she said out loud. The little cairn terrier looked up at her and wagged her stubby tail. The dog wasn't much help in this situation; whatever happened, Frankie would be happy. That was just who she was. Sure, she might miss Autumn coming home between shifts to let her out, but she would adjust to whatever the new schedule was quickly enough.

With a sigh, Autumn put the rag down and looked around the kitchen. It was spotless. She cleaned whenever she was worried, and the fact that her house was practically sparkling right now showed just how stressed she was by the decision she had to make.

Even if I go to the interview, there's no guarantee that I will get the job, she told herself. Audrey had made it clear that there would be multiple applicants. Many of them were probably more qualified than she was. She had mentioned the job offer to Nick the evening before but hadn't had much of a chance to gauge his reaction to it. He had simply promised that they could talk about it tomorrow, but now that tomorrow was here, she was nervous.

Nick had done so much for her. He had taken a chance in hiring her and had given her an opportunity that she never would have gotten otherwise. If she did take this job offer, what would he think of her? She was grateful to him for everything he had done and didn't want him to think that she had just been using him to get work.

"What am I going to do?" she groaned.

Grabbing the dishrag, she walked to the laundry room and tossed it in the washer. The house was clean, but she still had to sweep the porch and make sure that her gas grill was working. Whistling to Frankie, she walked over to the back door and let the dog outside, following the little terrier before shutting the door behind her. She went over to the small shed in the backyard and pulled out a push broom to begin sweeping the leaves and dirt off her stone patio. She had just finished checking that the propane container was hooked up to the grill and everything was working well when she heard a car door slam. Frankie started barking and dashed around the side of the house. Her guests had arrived.

Autumn followed the dog around the house and waved as she saw Alicia and her husband get out of their car. Alicia bent down to greet Frankie, who was dancing around joyfully.

"Come around the back," Autumn said. "I was just about to drag the lawn furniture out of the shed. You guys can help if you want."

"Darn it," Alicia joked. "We should have gotten here later and let Nick do all of the hard work."

"Well, you don't have to help; we can just eat on the ground if you would rather."

Her friend stuck out her tongue playfully, then grabbed her husband's hand and dragged him toward the side of the house. Frankie followed, still thrilled at the prospect of having guests. Autumn smiled. It was a beautiful spring day, and even though she had a lot on her mind, she was looking forward to spending the next few hours with friends.

They were still dragging the table and chairs out of the shed when Nick appeared around the side of the house.

"I saw your car out front," he said to Alicia. "When no one answered my knock at the front door, I figured you'd be around back."

"You guessed right," Autumn said. "I should probably go around front and make sure Bonnie finds the place okay. Did you bring the food?"

"Yep," Nick said. He held up a plastic bag. "Three different kinds of meat and both hotdog and hamburger buns."

"Great," Autumn said, grinning. "I have the drinks inside. Bonnie said that she would be bringing potato salad and pasta salad, so hopefully we're all set. I'll go get the drinks and wait for Bonnie, but you can go ahead and start cooking if you would like to."

She hummed as she mixed the lemonade and fruit punch inside. Simply being outdoors in the nice weather and seeing the people she cared most about had boosted her mood significantly. It was a good reminder that life was more than work. It was about the small, daily pleasures, and the relationships that she built.

A couple of minutes later, a knock at the front door signaled Bonnie's arrival. Bonnie was a friend of Alicia's, whom the other woman had met in her book club. Autumn had met her for the first time a few weeks ago, and had quickly become friends with the shy, quiet woman. Bonnie lived alone and had had terrible luck with men, but she was one of the kindest people that Autumn knew.

"Come on in," she called out. She waited, then a moment later put down the wooden spoon that she had been using to stir the lemonade and opened the door herself.

"Sorry," Bonnie said. "I heard something, but I wasn't sure if you said 'come in' or 'I'm coming'. I didn't want to open the door if I wasn't supposed to."

"That's fine," Autumn said. "Come in and make yourself at home. Everyone else is in the backyard."

"I brought food," Bonnie said, holding up two plastic covered bowls. "I hope it's good. I haven't made potato salad for a while."

"I'm sure it will be wonderful," Autumn said. "I'll take those and find serving spoons for them. You can go and join the others."

It wasn't until she brought all the food out, had the drinks set up, and a tablecloth thrown over the table that she got a chance to sit down and catch up with her friends. It was the first time they had all gotten together like this, though they had all met each other separately on various occasions.

"I can't believe how nice it is out," Alicia said. "It's the perfect weather for barbecuing. It's still early enough in the year that there aren't any bugs, but warm enough that we can actually enjoy being outside."

"I'll have to buy another citronella candle; it seemed to work pretty well to keep the mosquitoes away last year." Autumn smiled, thinking of the late summer nights she and Alicia had spent sitting on the porch, drinking wine and talking about their day. She couldn't have been happier that the weather was beginning to warm up. She had had more than enough of snow and cold to last her a lifetime.

"We aren't the only ones doing this today," Nick said. "When I stopped at the store, there were about five other people buying the same food I was."

"I'm glad you got there before they ran out of ground beef," Autumn said. "The grill already smells delicious."

"It will only be a couple of minutes until it's done," Nick told her. "In the meantime, why don't you tell us more about this job offer? It sounds like a great opportunity for you."

Autumn poured herself a cup of lemonade, then sighed. "It is… but I don't know if I'm going to take it. I love working at Asheville Meadows. There's no reason to change that."

"But, Autumn, this is what you have wanted to do for a long as I've known you," Alicia said. Behind her, Nick nodded.

"I think you should at least go to the interview," he said. "While I would love it if you stayed at Asheville Meadows for my own selfish reasons, I don't want to hold you back. You will always have a place there. I hope you know that."

Austin felt a lump in her throat and quickly took a sip of lemonade. "If you really think I should do it," she said slowly. "I guess I'll call her and see when she wants me to come in for the interview. Whatever happens, I won't leave Asheville Meadows without giving you plenty of warning."

She felt a tingle of excitement as she drained the rest of her glass of lemonade. She hadn't been looking for a new job; far from it, in fact, but now that the prospect of finally achieving her lifelong dream was at her fingertips, she couldn't help but wonder where this new opportunity might take her.

CHAPTER THREE

Blake's Steakhouse was in the next town over; a small village called Fox Landing. Autumn had never eaten there, but it was on her and Nick's shortlist for their date nights. She took a deep breath as she walked toward the restaurant's front doors, fighting down the feeling of anxiety that suddenly plagued her. What was she thinking? She had no idea how to be a real chef. Why was she even considering leaving Asheville Meadows, when she was so happy there?

Get a hold of yourself, she thought. *Even if she does offer the job to me, I don't have to take it. I can just tell her the truth; that I'm happy where I am.* Still, the anxiety didn't completely vanish as she walked through the doors. It was early in the day and the restaurant didn't open until after noon, and Autumn was glad that she wouldn't actually be cooking for any customers. It was bad enough that her food was going to be judged by the restaurant's owner as well as the staff and the other chef.

"Ms. Roth," someone said. "Or can I call you Autumn? I'm glad you made it. I hope the drive wasn't too bad."

"Autumn is fine," she said, turning to see Audrey Blake walking toward her. "It is only about a twenty-minute drive. It's not bad at all."

"Wonderful. We're still waiting for a couple of applicants to arrive. You can go wait in the kitchen with the others, if you'd like. The employee restrooms are through the door at the back of the kitchen; feel free to stop there if you need to use them. We've got the coffee machine running, and you can grab a bottle of water out of the fridge if you'd like. Go ahead and introduce yourself to everyone else. I'll be in once everyone is here."

Steeling herself to meet the people who were going to be competing for the position with her, as well as the staff that she might end up working with for the next couple of years, she followed the direction in which Audrey had pointed and let herself through a swinging door. What she found on the other side took her breath away. When she had first started working at Asheville Meadows, she had been impressed by the industrial kitchen, but the kitchen in Blake's Steakhouse dwarfed the one at the nursing home. Everything was made out of spotless, stainless steel. There were three towering refrigerators, and a heavy door that she guessed led to a walk-in meat freezer. There were multiple stovetops and ovens, an industrial grade vent in the middle of the room, bright lighting coming from the recessed overhead bulbs, and of course, ample counter space.

"Hey, come on in." The cheery voice made Autumn force herself to drag her gaze away from the set of expensive looking knives that were laid out and met the eyes of a young woman wearing a spotless black uniform. "I'm Kiki, and I'm one of the sous chefs. I'll be helping out today."

"Autumn Roth," Autumn said, shaking the other woman's hand. "It's nice to meet you."

"You too. You're from the nursing home, right?" Autumn nodded. "Ms. Blake told me all about you. There are four other people that are supposed to be applying for the position today as well. The two already here are Calvin Wilcox and Beatrice Lange. Calvin is a home economics teacher at the high school, and Beatrice makes meals for a charity during her off time."

Autumn stepped further into the room and shook hands with a balding, middle-aged man and a strawberry blonde-haired woman who was dressed all in pastels.

"So, Audrey is only interviewing people who have nonprofessional experience with cooking?"

"Sort of," Kiki said. "Some people, like you, do get paid for cooking, but no one she is interviewing today has worked in a regular restaurant, and no one has gone to a cooking school. Her whole thing is finding hidden talent."

"That's neat," Autumn said. "Well, I'm flattered to be here. It's nice to meet all of you."

"It's nice to meet you too," Beatrice said. "You cook at a nursing home? That must be interesting."

Autumn spent the next few minutes talking about her experiences at Asheville Meadows. By the time she was done, two new people had arrived; a young man named Drew Adler and an older man named Leonardo Dodd, but he insisted everyone called him Leo.

"Now that we are all here, why don't we get started on the interview portion?" Audrey said. "I'll call you each back into my office, and we can just go over your experience, your goals for the future, and any questions you may have. Then we will start cooking. Working in a professional kitchen is a high stress, very demanding job, and not everyone can do it. There's no shame in deciding that this job isn't for you. I know how hard it can be to find a good position in a kitchen without spending years at a school or getting experience in a similar environment, and I want to extend the same chance that my mentor gave me to one of you."

Autumn had to wait her turn while the two people who had arrived before her went in for their interviews. She was still nervous but realizing that she wasn't the only person who didn't have any experience working in a professional kitchen made her feel better. In fact, she probably had more experience than most of the other applicants did. The kitchen at Asheville Meadows might not be exactly like working in a restaurant, but it did give her a lot of experience when it came to preparing large amounts of food with a strict deadline.

"Autumn Roth," Audrey called from her office after what seemed like an eternity. Autumn stood up from the tall stool she had been sitting on and made her way toward the door. She took a deep breath, trying to calm herself down. *It's not like I need this job*, she told herself. *Even if I don't get offered the position for whatever reason, it will be okay. It doesn't mean I'm not good enough – I know I'm good enough. It just means I'm not the perfect fit for this specific place.*

"Go ahead and take a seat," Audrey said. "Tell me a bit about yourself. How long have you lived in town? What's your family like? Are you married? Any kids? I want to get to know the real you."

Autumn took a deep breath, then began answering the questions. She told Audrey about her family, her move to Asheville, the grocery store and how she had found her job at Asheville Meadows. By the time she was done, she felt more relaxed. Audrey was easy to talk to. She seemed to know how to put people at ease when she wanted to, though Autumn didn't doubt that she could be quite intimidating if the situation called for it.

"Thank you," Audrey said. "We're like a family here. It's important to me that everyone gets along well, and that we are all team players. This restaurant is my life, and I don't want any petty drama or personal vendettas getting in the way of business here. You seem like you'd be a great fit. We still have the next portion of the interview to get through, of course. I'll be asking each of you to create a three-course meal. You won't be given any instructions, but you will each be making the same basic dishes. The first course will be a green salad. The second will be a chicken entrée, and the third will be a chocolate cake. Whoever gets the position will be expected to create a lot of their own dishes, so I want to see your creativity at play here. Once everyone's done, we will all sit down and eat together. You will be asked to cook enough that everyone can get a small portion of your dish. After that, you will all be free to go home, and I will talk with Kiki and we will decide together who gets the position. Do you have any questions?"

"No," Autumn said. "That all makes sense."

"Wonderful," Audrey said. "When you return to the kitchen, send Drew in. Once I'm done talking to him, we'll get started."

CHAPTER FOUR

"Where's the basil?" Autumn muttered as she searched through the fridge. There was fresh sage, cilantro, oregano... "There you are," she said, grabbing the fresh basil leaves. She had decided to make a chicken pesto dish for her entrée course but wasn't completely sure whether or not it had been the right decision. She had seen two of the other applicants making chicken Alfredo dishes, and she had no idea what Leo was making – he was sequestered in the opposite corner from her.

She had finished making a light salad with lettuce, shredded carrots, shredded cucumber, and a white wine vinaigrette sauce, and as a last-second thought had added a sprinkle of crushed walnuts to it. She already had her cake in the oven – that had been an easy choice; she had simply made her favorite chocolate lava cake. There was vanilla ice cream in the freezer, and she knew that the gooey chocolate dessert couldn't go wrong.

She returned to her spot in the kitchen and finished making the pesto. The chicken breast was already cooking, and she had cauliflower boiling away on the stove. Instead of making mashed potatoes, she had decided for the lighter alternative of mashed cauliflower, which would be delicious with some butter, salt, pepper, and shredded cheese mixed in. She had been nervous when she first started cooking, but once she decided what she was going to make, most of her nerves had melted away, and she was simply cooking, like she did every day. Working almost on autopilot, she drained the cauliflower and began mashing it, adding the spices one by one. They weren't being timed, at least not officially, but Autumn had the feeling that it wouldn't look good if one of them took too much longer than the others. This was a restaurant, after all; being able to cook quickly was almost as important as being able to cook well. If the dish took too long to get out, then they would have unhappy guests.

Ten minutes later, Autumn scooped the last of the mashed cauliflower into a serving bowl and set the dish on the counter. She went down a mental checklist in her head. Everything was complete. Breathing a sigh of relief, she glanced to the side. The only one still cooking was Drew, and it looked like he was almost done as well.

"That looks wonderful," Beatrice said. She was peeking over Autumn's shoulder. "I can't wait to taste it. I wish I had been a little bit more original, but I decided to just stick with making what I know. Have you seen what Leo is making? I'm allergic to a couple of things, and I like to keep an eye on what ingredients people are using."

Autumn shook her head. "I haven't been over to his side of the room."

"Well, I'm not sure what it is, but it looks like it belongs in a five-star restaurant. I was never that good at presentation, and I think that's going to be my weak point."

Beatrice walked away to finish putting the last touches on her food. Autumn was left to stare at her chicken pesto and mashed cauliflower. She hadn't even thought about presentation. She didn't have any decorative herbs laid out, or any colorful spices sprinkled over the food. She had made it just like she was used to cooking at the nursing home; quality food, but it was just placed on a platter and forgotten about until someone was ready to eat it.

Beside her, Drew stepped back and untied his apron. He was done, which meant that she didn't have any time to improve the presentation of her food. It would just have to do.

She untied her own apron and hung it up, glancing over at Leo as she did so. She realized suddenly that

Leo hadn't been interviewed by Audrey. He had been the last one to arrive, and she hadn't learned much about him besides his name. *What's his story?* she wondered.

"It looks like everyone's done," Kiki said in her perpetually cheerful voice. "The five of you can go sit down at one of the tables. Audrey and I are going to go over your dishes visually right now, then we'll bring them out and we can all eat. First, though, feel free to take a look at what everyone else has made. A good chef never stops getting inspiration, and besides, it's always fun to see what other people come up with."

The five of them filed around the room, each of them shooting nervous glances at each other's dishes. Autumn was the only one who had made a pesto dish. Beatrice and Drew had both made variances of chicken Alfredo, and Calvin had made breaded chicken Parmesan with marinara sauce. Leo's dish was something exotic looking that Autumn couldn't place off the top of her head. The chicken breast had been sautéed in some sort of brown sauce and had sprigs of cilantro placed carefully on top. It smelled delicious and looked even better.

Autumn glanced back at her own food and her breath caught as she saw Beatrice knock into the bowl containing the mashed cauliflower. She exhaled when the other woman reached around and caught it before it could crash to the floor. She wondered suddenly if she should be worried about one of the other applicants trying to sabotage her food. They had all gotten along well so far, but she realized that they were each in competition for the position. *It's too late now,* she thought, deciding not to worry about it.

The five of them filed out of the kitchen and took a seat around one of the larger tables. All of them were silent; the casual chatting from earlier in the morning gone as they considered their dishes and, if they were anything like Autumn, thinking about all of the changes they wished they had made.

It wasn't long until Kiki and Audrey came out of the kitchen, bearing platters of food. They started with the salads. Each of them got five small bowls with a portion of each salad inside. Autumn tried hers first. It wasn't bad; the walnuts added a lot, but she wished that she had thought to put some dried cranberries in as well. They would have added more texture, and just a dash of sweetness. The other salads ranged from basic – Beatrice's was simply baby spinach leaves, almond slivers, and balsamic vinaigrette – to exquisite. Leo's was her favorite. He had shredded iceberg lettuce, cucumbers, carrots, red cabbage, and had added crunchy rice noodles as well. Over the top, he had drizzled a sweet ginger dressing. She made a note to ask him how he had made the dressing, because she didn't remember seeing it in the fridge.

Next came the main courses. After tasting hers, Autumn was satisfied with it. While it didn't have the same impressive presentation as Leo's dish did, it tasted amazing. There was something a little bit off about the cauliflower dish, but she couldn't put her finger on it and was too distracted by the rest of the food to pay much attention to it.

The other dishes were all quite good as well. Beatrice's tasted like something that Autumn's grandmother might have made. It was homey and comforting. The chicken Parmesan dish was one of the best that Autumn had ever had, but once again it was Leo's dish that won her over. The chicken had been cooked in a sweet teriyaki sauce, and the sprigs of cilantro both made the dish look nice, and added a fresh, crisp taste.

Dessert was the only course where Autumn was confident that her dish was the best. The chocolate lava cake was moist and perfectly gooey on the inside. Combined with the vanilla ice cream, it was a dessert to die for.

"Well, that was quite the meal," Audrey said. "I want to thank everyone for coming in. Kiki and I will –"

Audrey broke off midsentence as Leo began to cough. He pounded at his chest, leaning over the table as he gasped for air. Concerned, Autumn began to stand up, but then sat back down again; she had no idea what to do.

Wheezing, Leo looked up at them. Autumn saw a red rash on his neck. His eyes met hers, then his breath caught, and his face began turning purple as he scratched at his neck, unable to draw in air.

Feeling frozen, Autumn could do nothing but watch as Beatrice leapt up and helped Leo to the floor. She was the only one out of all of them that seemed to have her wits about her as she tilted his head back and began attempting to give him CPR. After a couple of seconds, Kiki jumped up and ran to the other room. Autumn heard beeping as she made a call on the restaurant's landline. Feeling helpless, and not wanting to get in Beatrice's way, Autumn kept to her seat, staring at Leo. She kept waiting for him to start breathing on his own again, but he had fallen frighteningly still.

CHAPTER FIVE

Autumn stared blankly at the ambulance through the restaurant's front doors. The doors had been propped open to allow the paramedics to come and go freely. She had watched as they gave Leo an antihistamine injection, but it had been too late. She had seen the moment that they had stopped trying. Now, they were wheeling him out of the building on a shrouded stretcher. No one knew what had happened to Leo. Had he had a heart attack? She wondered. He had been older, but he had seemed so healthy. The way he had been gasping for air made Autumn think that he might have choked on something, but that rash that had appeared on his neck didn't fit with that idea.

The other applicants were all sitting stunned, staring either at the place where Leo's body had been, or watching the ambulance, like Autumn was. Kiki was talking to one of the police officers, and Audrey was nowhere to be seen.

"Can I have your name, please?"

Autumn blinked and turned her head to see a young police officer standing next to her.

"Autumn Roth," she said. "I was here for a job interview."

The officer nodded. "The owner told me all about it. If you take a seat with the others, we will call you for questioning in a couple of minutes."

"Okay." Autumn started for the table, then paused. "What... what happened?" She asked. "Did the paramedics say anything?"

"I don't know anything," he said apologetically. "I'm just supposed to get everyone's name."

She nodded. Knowing that asking any further questions would be useless, she sat down at the table with the remaining three applicants. Beatrice had her hands pressed to her mouth, was rocking back and forth slowly with a horrified expression on her face. Calvin was staring blankly down at the table, and Drew kept glancing toward the place where Leo's body had fallen. None of them spoke to Autumn as she sat down.

"It's all my fault," she heard Beatrice mutter softly to herself.

"It's not," Autumn said. "You're the only one that even tried to save him. The rest of us were frozen. Don't blame yourself."

The other woman ignored her, seemingly too horrified to respond. Autumn didn't blame her; they were all in shock.

Autumn jolted when she heard her name a few minutes later. She kept replaying Leo's death over and over in her mind, looking for a possible cause. It had just happened so quickly. It had been completely without warning, and try as she might, she couldn't think of a single thing that might have caused it.

"Autumn?" She jumped when her name was called.

"Right here," she said. She headed over to the young female detective who would be questioning her. Her fingers felt cold, and she was beginning to feel sick to her stomach.

"I'm Officer Tidwell. I'm just going to ask you a few questions about what happened today. Let's start with how well you knew the deceased."

"I had just met him today," she said. "He was here to apply for the same job that I was."

The young officer nodded and made a note on her notepad. "Would you say this is a particularly competitive position?"

Autumn blinked. "I suppose so. The owner is the one that approached all of us. I don't think any of us need this job to make ends meet; we all have our own professions and hobbies right now. But we are all passionate about cooking, and this is a once-in-a-lifetime opportunity for all of us."

"Did Mr. Dodd speak with you at all during the interview process?"

"He introduced himself to me, but that's about it," Autumn said. She thought back, trying to remember if she and Leo had exchanged any words. "I think he complimented me on the cake, right before he started choking."

"You said choking... did he have something caught in his throat? Did anyone attempt to perform the Heimlich maneuver?"

"No," Autumn said. "I guess I shouldn't have said he was choking. I really don't know what happened. He started coughing, and his breathing became wheezy, then his face started to turn purple and he collapsed. He also had a rash on his neck."

"Was he served separately from the rest of you? Did he eat anything that you didn't?"

"No," Autumn said. "We all ate the same things. We each made a three-course dinner, and then got to taste part of each dish."

"Who served him?"

"It was either Audrey or Kiki," Autumn said. "I'm sorry, but I don't remember which one it was." She had been too focused on her own success or failure to pay attention to anything else.

"Thank you. I think that's all we need. I'll just take your contact information, and if we need anything else, we will call you."

"Am I free to leave?" Autumn asked.

"You are, however, everything in the kitchen is going to be considered evidence. An officer will escort you to your purse, so you can retrieve your car keys and phone, but you're going to have to leave the rest of the contents of your purse along with your coat and any other personal belongings here."

Autumn paled. She didn't mind leaving the rest of her stuff behind – as long as she had her keys, her wallet, and her cell phone, she would be fine – but the fact that they were keeping evidence behind meant that they must think Leo's death hadn't been an accident. Were they looking for something in particular, or were they just being thorough?

She mulled over the question while she followed the police officer into the kitchen to get her keys, her phone, and her wallet. The officer watched her carefully, making sure that she didn't remove anything else from the purse. She looked around, wondering what it was that the police would be looking for. Calvin and Beatrice had both brought light jackets, though Autumn hadn't bothered. She wondered if the police would find anything incriminating in their pockets. Was it possible that one of them had wanted the job badly enough to poison Leo? It was true that he was the obvious winner out of the five of them. His food had tasted amazing, and he was also much better at presentation than any of them had been.

Feeling naked without her purse, Autumn walked through the restaurant, not meeting Beatrice's, Calvin's, or Drew's eyes. If one of them was a killer, she wanted to keep her distance. She slipped through the restaurant's front doors, nodding to the police officer that was guarding it, and took a single step toward the parking lot, only to realize that she wasn't the only one outside of the restaurant. Audrey was sitting on a bench next to the doors, sobbing quietly into her hands. Autumn hesitated, wondering if she should go to the other woman, then decided against it. What comfort could she possibly offer? No, it was better to let Audrey work through her grief by herself. For all she knew, Audrey might consider Autumn a suspect. She didn't know if the police had told the restaurant owner anything more than they had told her, but she wouldn't be surprised if Audrey had come to the same conclusion that she had; the police were treating Leo's death as something more than an accident.

CHAPTER SIX

Autumn woke up the next morning before her alarm went off, feeling depressed and out of sorts. The fact that she had seen someone die the day before weighed heavily on her. She hadn't heard anything from the police yet and knew that even if they did need to ask her more questions, she wouldn't learn anything new about the investigation unless they wanted her to. For all she knew, she was a suspect.

Even Frankie's happy attitude couldn't cheer her up. She went through the routine of letting the dog out, making coffee, and getting ready for work, but her heart wasn't in any of it. All she wanted was answers. Until she knew why Leo had died, she doubted she would be able to think of anything else. If he had simply had a heart attack or another medical emergency, his death would still be sad, but at least she would know that none of the other applicants had killed him. She had liked them all, and found it disturbing to think that she could like someone willing to commit a murder. It made her question her own judgment of character, and it was uncomfortable to think that a seemingly normal person could commit such a serious crime, and not act any differently after.

While lying in bed the night before, she had decided that even if Audrey still decided to offer the position to one of them, and on the off chance that Audrey decided that Autumn was the best fit, she would turn down the position anyway. She didn't want to spend the next few years of her life walking past the spot where Leo had died every single evening. She was beginning to wish that she had never even accepted the offer to go in for an interview.

This wasn't her first close encounter with death, but it wasn't getting any easier. She didn't think that she would ever be able to take something like this in stride, and she didn't want to. Life was precious, and each and every person had their own dreams, goals, and future. She couldn't stop thinking about Leo, and his family, if he had any. Their lives would have all changed in an instant when Leo hit the floor.

Autumn tossed a dog cookie to Frankie and stepped out the front door, locking it behind her. She was glad that she had to go in to Asheville Meadows today. Spending time around the people who had started to feel like family to her would be good. She didn't like being alone with such heavy thoughts weighing on her mind.

Autumn fought back a yawn as she walked through the nursing home's front doors. She had gotten poor sleep the night before and knew that she would pay for it that evening. Still, it felt good to walk into the familiar, warmly lit entranceway. It was early enough that only a couple of residents were up and about. She waved to a pair of elderly women who were sitting in the common area, then made a beeline for the kitchen. She had dug an old purse out of her closet, since her favorite one was still at the restaurant, and it was this that she set down on the counter. She would go to the staff room soon, but first, she wanted to see what was on the menu for the day.

Before she could grab the month's menu, she heard a soft rap at the kitchen door. She turned to see Nick standing there, an unusually grim expression on his face. Her stomach clenched. Had something happened to one of the residents during the night?

"Autumn, could you come with me?"

She nodded, grabbing her purse and following Nick out of the kitchen, toward the staff room. Her thoughts went immediately to her aunt and uncle, but she forced herself to calm down, telling herself that if something had happened to one of them, Nick would have called her immediately; he wouldn't have waited until she got to work.

"Go ahead and sit down," he said when they reached his office. He shut the door gently behind them. Autumn settled herself in the comfortable seat and waited as he took his own chair on the other side of the desk.

"Have you seen the news this morning?" he asked her.

"No," Autumn said. She hadn't wanted to be reminded of what had happened the day before. She already couldn't get it out of her head.

"Well, the reporter is saying that that man – Leo – was poisoned."

Autumn bit her lip. She had told Nick about Leo's death the evening before but hadn't gone into detail about it. She wondered whether the reporter had learned something about the case from the police, or if she was simply embellishing the tale to get more interest in it.

"Unfortunately, your name has been leaked as one of the possible suspects, along with the other people that were there."

"What?" Autumn exclaimed. "Nick, you know I wouldn't –"

"Of course I know you didn't have anything to do with it," Nick said, looking tired. "The only problem is, not everyone knows you as well as I do. When I walked in this morning, there were three separate messages on the answering machine from relatives of some of the residents here, expressing their concern that you were still cooking in the kitchen. Since I've been here, two more calls have come in. I hate to do this, but I'm going to have to ask you to take a leave of absence until this whole thing blows over. I know it's unfair but making sure the nursing home runs smoothly is my responsibility, and I don't want to cause anyone here concern when I don't have to. You're welcome to come and visit me and your aunt and uncle, of course, but you will have to stay out of the kitchen. We will keep paying you, and I'm sure this won't last too long. As soon as the police figure out what really happened, you will be free to go back to work."

Autumn stared at him, trying to sort through the emotions that were whirling around inside of her. She was angry, though she didn't want to admit it to Nick. He was right; it was his job to protect the nursing home. She knew that he didn't want to hurt her, and he was only doing this because he thought it was best. She was also hurt that any of the residents' relatives thought that she was a killer. Not only that, but they were concerned that she might poison the people here, the very people she had come to care so much about. *They don't know you*, she told herself. *To them, you are just a name and a face. All they have to go on is what they see on the news.*

She took a deep breath. "Okay," she said, ashamed at how shaky her voice was. "I'll just go home, I suppose."

Her voice caught on the last word, and, horrified, she felt her eyes fill with tears. Nick pushed his chair back and stood up, coming around the desk to lay a hand on her shoulder.

"Don't be ridiculous," he said. "I'm not going to kick you out of here and expect you to spend the day all by yourself after what happened. Let's go get coffee, then we can pick up some takeout for lunch and come back here and eat with your aunt and uncle in their room. I hate having to do this, Autumn. If it was up to me, and if I wasn't risking the residents here getting pulled out by their relatives, I would just ignore everyone who doubts you."

"I know," she said. "I'm sorry. I don't mean to cry. It's just one more thing, on top of everything else, and it's too much."

"Come on," he said. "Let's go get coffee. You'll feel better with some caffeine and good pastries inside of you. Food always brightens you up."

CHAPTER SEVEN

The next few days were hard. Without work, Autumn realized just how little she had to fill her time. She took a handful of long walks with Frankie, cleaned the house far more deeply than she ever had before, went shopping, and spent more time with Alicia. At first, she had hoped that the case would be solved quickly, but she was still being forced to stay away from work by the next Monday. Wondering what would happen if Leo's death was never solved, she began to feel a gnawing panic. She was glad when a phone call from Alicia interrupted her simple lunch.

"Are you free today? Bonnie and I are going to head to the book sale at the library, if you want to come."

"Sure," Autumn said, trying to disguise the relief in her voice. "Just tell me when we're meeting, and I'll be there."

Both Alicia and Bonnie were avid readers, and though Autumn enjoyed completing the occasional book, she tended to spend more of her time watching television. Somehow it was easier for her to get into the visual aspect of TV shows than it was for her to get deeply involved in a book. Still, she figured she might be able to pick up some old cooking books, and she would enjoy spending time with her friends, regardless.

The Asheville library was a small building near the park in the center of town. Autumn parked next to Alicia's car and got out, looking around for her friends. She spotted the two women by the library doors and made a beeline for them.

"Hey," Alicia said. "How are you doing?"

"I've been better," Autumn said with a sigh.

"Still no word from the police?"

"Nope. I have no idea what's going on with the case. Nick thinks it's still too soon for me to come back to work, so I'm stuck doing nothing."

"I don't know," Bonnie said. "It doesn't sound too bad to me. You get to spend your time at home, but you're still getting paid. I would love that."

"Maybe it would be different if I had an exact date that I would be able to go back to work. I just can't help but wonder what will happen if the case is never closed and Nick never decides that it's okay for me to start working again without raising a panic. I don't want to have to find a new job. I love cooking. I love everything about Asheville Meadows. I just keep kicking myself for ever going on the interview."

"Don't do that," Alicia said. "There's no way you could have known what was going to happen. I think it's good that you took the chance and reached for your dreams. You still might get the position, you know. I doubt the restaurant will close down because of this, especially if the police end up determining that it was an accident."

"I don't want the position anymore," Autumn said. "I just want to go back to work at Asheville Meadows. I know I'm happy there, and I won't have to think of Leo's death every time I go to my job."

"I think you're being dramatic," Alicia said, putting her hands on her hips. "You always wanted to work in a restaurant, Autumn. This is an amazing opportunity. You know, people are going to die at the nursing home eventually too. What are you going to do then? If the restaurant owner offers you the job, I think you should take it. I don't want you to settle for something short of your dream just because you are afraid of change."

Autumn stared at her friend, at a loss for words. As always, Alicia had a point, and she wasn't afraid to say it.

"I think you should do whatever will make you happiest in the long run," Bonnie said. "Where do you want to be in five years? When you envision the future, are you at Asheville Meadows, or are you at a fancy restaurant? Dreams can change. If you're happy where you are, and you don't feel bored there, then I don't see why you should leave. As long as you enjoy what you're doing, why change it?"

Both of her friends had good points. Autumn sighed, not wanting to think about all of it just then.

"Let's go in and look for books," she said. "If we don't hurry, all of the good ones will be gone."

Alicia and Bonnie didn't let her off the hook that easily. After they were done purchasing their books from the library sale, the three of them went to the coffee shop to talk and compare their purchases. Autumn had picked up a couple of cooking books, including a healthy low sodium, low-fat book that she thought she might store in the kitchen at Asheville Meadows. She realized, staring at the cover, that she had bought it without even thinking about her current work situation. Some part of her seemed confident that she was going to go back there.

"I love these sales," Bonnie said. "I got two bags of books for ten dollars. Hey, Autumn, do you want to trade with me? I'll sit at home all day and get paid while you do my job. That's probably the only way I'll be able to get through all these books before the end of the year."

Autumn chuckled. "Somehow, I don't think the mayor's office would be okay with that trade," she said. "At least it would give me something useful to do, though. I'm going stir crazy."

"You need a hobby," Alicia declared. "Something besides cooking."

"Like what?" Autumn asked.

"I have no idea. That's up to you. You could start doing crafting with me. Maybe if I have someone helping me, my little business will finally take off."

"My creativity begins and ends in the kitchen," Autumn said. "I can't paint or knit worth anything."

"Well, that's not much help," Alicia said. "Maybe the restaurant will call you soon, then you can quit moping around and get to work."

Autumn sighed again. "I told you, I don't think I'm going to take the job even if it is offered. Besides, I wasn't even the best applicant. Leo –" she broke off. Leo was dead. Without him there, she very well might be the best applicant.

"Leo was the best?" Alicia asked, raising her eyebrows. "Do you think one of the other people might have killed him, so they could get the position?"

"It's possible," Autumn said. "I have a feeling that's what the police think happened."

"Does that mean you might be in danger?" Alicia wondered. "I'm sure you were one of the best there, besides him. If you get offered the position, you might be a target for the killer."

That was something that Autumn hadn't thought of. She felt goosebumps on her skin. "That's just another reason for me not to accept the job," she said. "Following my dreams isn't worth getting killed for."

"I can't argue with that," her friend said. "Maybe you're right. If they don't solve the case, I think you should stay far away from that restaurant. You need to be careful. If something happened to you, I don't know what I would do. I've never lost a friend before, and I don't want to start now."

After that, the conversation turned to lighter subjects. Autumn knew that Alicia had spooked herself by talking about Autumn possibly being a target. All the talk of death had caused Bonnie to be unusually quiet, and Autumn herself was left to ponder the fact that she might be in danger.

When her cell phone rang, she was almost glad of the interruption. The number was an unfamiliar one, but it was local. Feeling a spark of hope that it might be the police, she excused herself from the table and got up to answer it.

"Hello?"

"Autumn? This is Audrey Blake, from the restaurant."

"Oh, hi," Autumn said. "Have you heard from the police yet?"

"Yes," the other woman said. "They called here just a few minutes ago. They have finished going through the evidence, and I'm able to open the kitchen again. You and the other applicants are also welcome to come back and get your stuff."

"That's wonderful," Autumn said. "Does this mean that they have solved the case?"

"I don't think so. I think they just have everything they needed from the kitchen. I'll be at the restaurant in about two hours. If you want to stop by then, you're welcome to."

"I'll be there," Autumn said. She was eager to get her purse, along with all of the makeup and knickknacks that she had in there, back, and she also wanted another chance to talk to Audrey in person.

She wanted to know more about what the police had said to the other woman. If they were getting close to solving the case, then that could only be good news.

CHAPTER EIGHT

"All of your stuff is still in the kitchen," Audrey said. "Kiki is back there to make sure nothing gets messed up – not worse than it already is, at least. Beatrice is here already, and Calvin should be arriving soon."

"Thanks," Autumn said. "I'll hurry."

She hadn't expected the other applicants to be there, though she should have guessed that they might have all gotten the same call from Audrey. While she was eager to talk to the restaurant owner, she wasn't so eager to talk to the other applicants. If one of them had killed Leo, then she didn't want to be anywhere nearby. *I'll just be quick*, she told herself.

She made her way to the kitchen and let herself through the swinging door. Kiki greeted her when she walked inside. "Everything is about where everyone left it," she said. "The police moved a few things around, but the mess isn't too bad. Just grab whatever is yours."

"Thanks," Autumn said. "How are you doing? This must be hard for everyone who works at the restaurant."

"It is," Kiki said. "We've all been questioned a few times. We –"

She broke off as the sound of a commotion reached their ears. Someone was arguing in the dining area Autumn had just left. Curious, she pushed the swinging door open and saw two police officers standing in front of Audrey.

"You said you were done with the kitchen," Audrey was saying angrily. "I don't see why you want to go back in."

"We need a sample of your sesame oil," the officer said. "We have a warrant –"

"Fine, go ahead," Audrey said angrily. "But don't make a mess. I just got done tidying up."

Autumn stepped back as the police walked toward the doors. They pushed open the swinging door and stepped into the kitchen, seeming surprised to find her and Beatrice there.

"Sesame oil?" one of the officers asked Kiki. The sous chef led them to the pantry. The remaining officer looked between Calvin, Beatrice, and Autumn.

"Is one of you Autumn Roth?" he asked after a moment.

"I am," Autumn said, puzzled. "Why?"

"I guess we're killing two birds with one stone," he muttered. "We are going to need to bring you down to the station for questioning. If you come with us willingly, it will be a lot easier than if we have to pick up a warrant."

"Of course I'll come willingly," Autumn said. "Just let me grab my bag."

A few minutes later, her purse in hand, she found herself in the back of a police vehicle. Audrey, Kiki, Beatrice, and Calvin had all watched her go. It had been one of the most embarrassing moments in Autumn's life. She had no idea what the police wanted with her. Out of everyone at the restaurant, she was the only one that she knew for a fact was innocent.

At the police station, she was led to a small room with a sturdy table and three chairs. She took a seat and put her purse on the table, glancing up at the slowly ticking clock on the wall. It was five minutes before she heard a soft rap on the door, and someone came into the room.

"I'm Detective Wendel," he said. "I'll be handling the case from here on out. Do you know why you're here?"

"I don't have any idea," Autumn said. "They just told me that I needed to come back to the station with them. What's going on?"

"A week ago, you were at Blake's Steakhouse applying for a job, is that correct?" he asked.

"Yes," she said. "I'm sure you already have that on record. I was questioned right after Leo died."

"We do," he said. "I just want to make sure everything is clear. Could you tell me what dishes you made during the working part of the interview?"

"I made a salad with a white wine vinaigrette dressing, pesto chicken with mashed cauliflower, and a chocolate lava cake."

"Could you tell me the ingredients you used in the mashed cauliflower dish?"

"Cauliflower, salted butter, black pepper, salt, and some shredded Parmesan cheese. I also added a small amount of cream cheese to improve the texture."

"Did you add any oils?"

"Oils?" Autumn asked, confused. "Like olive oil? No."

"Could you explain why we found sesame oil in your cauliflower dish?"

"Sesame oil?" Autumn blinked at him. Suddenly the odd flavor she had noted in the cauliflower dish made sense. She had hardly thought about it at the time, but now that the detective had pointed out to her, she knew that she had recognized the flavor.

"Did you know Mr. Dodd?"

"I already told you, I didn't know him at all. The first time I met him was that day. Why would there be sesame oil in the mashed cauliflower?"

"That's what we're trying to figure out," the man said. "Tell us about your current job."

"I work at Asheville Meadows, the nursing home."

"Are you happy there?"

"I love it there," she said firmly.

"Why were you looking for a different job, then?"

"I've always wanted to be a professional chef. My friends convinced me to try out for the position. If I didn't get it, I would just go back to working at Asheville Meadows. It wouldn't have been a big deal. I wasn't even sure if I would take the position if it did get offered to me."

"I think that's about it," the man said, frowning as he made marks on his notepad. "First though, could you tell me if anyone else had access to your cooking?"

"Everyone did," Autumn said. "We all walked around and looked at each other's dishes, then the applicants left the kitchen while Kiki and Mrs. Blake judged them privately." She suddenly remembered seeing Beatrice almost knock the cauliflower dish off of the counter. Before she could mention it to the detective, he had changed the subject. "Who would be best to call if we wanted to speak with someone at your current job?"

"Nicholas Holt," she said. "He's the director of Asheville Meadows." With a twinge of worry, she remembered that she had been asked not to work temporarily. "I'm taking a leave of absence from there," she admitted. "It didn't start until after Leo's death, though. Nick was getting concerned calls from some of the relatives of the residents there and asked me to step down until the case was closed."

"I appreciate your honesty," the detective said. "I think that's it. You're free to go. If you think of anything else that might be relevant, give me a call directly. Here's my card. My personal number's on the back."

"Thank you," she said. She hesitated a moment, then took a deep breath. "Am... am I a suspect?"

"Ms. Roth," the detective said, "as of right now, everyone who was in that restaurant the day of the murder is a suspect."

CHAPTER NINE

The police brought her back to the restaurant, where, exhausted and wanting nothing more than to talk with her friends, Autumn found Beatrice waiting by her car.

"Oh, good," the other woman said. "I was hoping they would bring you back soon. What did they say?"

Autumn tensed, frowning. "I'm not sure if I should say anything," she said. "The police probably want to keep the details about the case private."

"Oh, did they tell you not to talk to anyone?" Beatrice asked.

"Well, no," Autumn admitted.

"Did they say something about sesame oil?" the other woman asked, her voice a whisper. Surprised, Autumn blinked.

"How did you know about that?"

"I was there when the police officers came looking for the restaurant's sesame oil, remember?" she asked.

"Oh, right."

"I want to talk about all of this, but I don't want to do it here. Can we go get coffee or something?"

"Why do you want to talk to *me*?" Autumn asked. "The police just took me in for questioning. How do you know *I'm* not the killer?"

"You have no reason to want to hurt Leo," Beatrice said. "You don't even know who he was, do you?"

"Who he was?" Autumn said, feeling more out of the loop than ever.

"Things are starting to make sense to me," Beatrice said, not answering her question. "I'm not sure who to trust, though. Please, can we go talk somewhere?"

Autumn sighed, then agreed. She and Beatrice made plans to meet at a small coffee shop in Fox Landing. She got into her car and started the engine, wondering what she was getting herself into. Why didn't Beatrice just talk to the police if she thought she knew something?

"Sorry for all the secrecy," Beatrice said it once they were seated at the coffee shop. "I just don't know who might have been the one to kill him, and I don't want to risk the wrong person overhearing us."

"I understand," Autumn said. "What did you mean about me not knowing who Leo was?"

"Well, I thought he seemed familiar while we were at the interview, so when I got home later I looked the restaurant up online, and I realized that he was one of the long-term chefs there."

"That doesn't make any sense," Autumn said. "If he already worked there, then why was he applying?" Even as she spoke, she realized that that would explain why Audrey hadn't brought him into her office for an interview, and why he had seemed to know his way around the kitchen so well. It would also explain Audrey's extreme reaction to his death.

"I don't know for sure, but I think that Audrey must have wanted him in there with us to see how we work when we think we're unsupervised. She wasn't in there watching us, after all. And he would have had to work with whoever got hired, so I'm sure he wanted to have input in it. If we knew he was one of the people deciding whether or not we got hired for the job, then we might act differently around him, but as another applicant, he would have been able to see us as we really are."

"That's smart," Autumn said. "I think you're onto something."

"It just makes sense. But that's not why I wanted to meet here. It's about the sesame oil."

"What about it?" Autumn asked. "I don't see how it could have anything to do with Leo's death." Once again, she remembered how Beatrice had bumped against the bowl of mashed cauliflower. Had she made a mistake in meeting the other woman here? If something had been added to the cauliflower dish, then Beatrice must have been the one to do it.

"Well, you see, I'm deathly allergic to sesame seeds," Beatrice said. "And the thing is… I told Audrey about that during my interview with her."

Autumn blinked. "You're allergic to sesame seeds? But if there was sesame oil in the cauliflower, why didn't you react to it?"

"I don't like cauliflower," Beatrice admitted. "I didn't taste any of the mashed cauliflower dish. I knew I wouldn't like it, and I didn't want to look like I was being rude if I had to try to choke them down."

"Leo must have been allergic to sesame oil as well," Autumn said. "But none of us would have known that."

"None of us besides Audrey or Kiki," Beatrice said quietly.

Autumn fell silent. It was a chilling thought. Had Audrey or Kiki poisoned the food with sesame oil in order to kill Leo, or had Beatrice been the real target? Or maybe the truth was something else, something even more sinister.

"Did you tell anyone else about your allergy?" she asked.

"No, I didn't. I just watched the ingredients that everyone was using. I made sure no one added any sesame oil in. Even if I had accidentally ingested some, I have an EpiPen in my purse. I would get hives first, which would alert me to what was happening with enough time to go get the pen before my throat started to swell. But everyone's reaction is different. The way Leo was having difficulty breathing, and his rash… That could have been an allergic reaction."

"We really should go to the police with this," Autumn said. "Someone was trying to kill either you or Leo. The fact that Audrey and Kiki are the only ones who could have known will narrow it down for them."

"You don't think that I'm crazy?" Beatrice asked. "I don't want to waste their time."

"It won't be a waste of their time," Autumn said. "I think this could really help them."

"If you think it's best, then that's what we'll do," Beatrice said. "I'm going to run to the restroom. We can make the call when I get back."

Autumn waited until the other woman was out of sight before she pulled out her cell phone and dialed the number on the card the detective had given her.

"This is Autumn Roth," she said when he answered. "We're at the little coffee shop on the corner of Main Street in Fox Landing. I'm with one of the other people that applied for the job, and I think she might be the killer."

The police walked in shortly after Beatrice sat back down. At first the other woman watched them with a puzzled expression, but it quickly turned to shock when the two officers approached their table.

"Ms. Lange?" one of them said. "You're going to have to come with us."

"W-why?" she stuttered.

"You're wanted for questioning in relation to the murder of Leonardo Dodd."

Autumn flinched and looked away when Beatrice shot her a betrayed look. She didn't know if calling the police was the right thing to do, but it all added up. Beatrice must have known about Leo's allergy somehow. She had been the one to bump into the cauliflower bowl before it had been served. She hadn't eaten any of the mashed cauliflower, and Autumn knew that she desperately wanted the job. Beatrice must have known that she wouldn't be good enough to get the job if there was only one position open, but if Audrey suddenly found herself out of a second chef, then she just might have a chance.

If I'm wrong, Autumn thought, *I'm really going to regret this later.*

CHAPTER TEN

"Welcome back, Ms. Roth," Emily said cheerfully when she found Autumn in the kitchen at Asheville Meadows on Wednesday morning.

"I told you, call me Autumn," Autumn said, smiling. "And it's good to be back."

The day before, the news reporter said that an arrest had been made in relation to Leonardo's case, and the news screen had flashed to a mug shot of Beatrice. The woman had been arrested, and the case was closed, which meant that Autumn was free to return to work.

Breakfast at the nursing home was always the easiest meal. Cereal, oatmeal, eggs, and either sausage or turkey bacon were the normal staples. On the weekends, they often had pancakes or waffles. Today, she and Emily spent half an hour making scrambled eggs and heating up the oatmeal before throwing the bacon on to cook. It was her first day back in a week, and Autumn felt a level of peace that she hadn't in all the days that she had been forced to sit at home. While the look that Beatrice had given her as the police marched her away still haunted her, she knew that she had made the right decision.

As the residents began to trickle into the dining room, she took orders and marched food out of the kitchen. Once everyone had a bowl or a plate in front of them, she served herself a plate of bacon and eggs and went to join her aunt and uncle.

Uncle Al and Aunt Lucy were Autumn's greatest source of emotional support. Her mother lived only a couple of hours away, and visited a couple of times each year, but her and Autumn's relationship was strained. In many ways, her aunt and uncle were the caring parental figures she had never had.

"I'm glad you're back," Uncle Al said when she sat down across from him. "It just isn't the same here without you around."

Her aunt nudged her uncle with her good arm and gave him a sharp look. He chuckled and patted her wrist.

"Your aunt is right. I shouldn't be making you feel guilty about being gone. If that job offer is still on the table, I don't want you to think you can't take it because of us. We were just fine before you started working here, and as long as you keep visiting us, we'll be fine if you decide to move onto greener pastures."

"Don't worry, I won't be taking the job even if it gets offered to me," Autumn said. She shook a couple of drops of hot sauce onto her eggs before taking a bite.

"Why not?" her uncle asked.

"I'm happy here, and I don't know if I would even like working there. Why should I make a change if I'm already happy where I am?"

"'Don't fix it if it isn't broken'?" her uncle chuckled. "I've never believed in that saying. If the great minds of the world lived by that idea, we wouldn't have half the things we have today. People were getting by just fine before we invented the light bulb, automobiles, and electricity, but life is certainly better now, isn't it?"

"What if I go there and I hate it, though?" Autumn asked.

"Then come back here," her uncle said. "But I think whatever you do, Autumn, you'll be happy, especially if you're cooking."

Left with her uncle's words to mull over, she helped clean up the breakfast dishes then drove home to let

Frankie out and take the dog on a short walk around the block. She inhaled deeply, enjoying the fresh spring air. Maybe her uncle was right. She had never been truly unhappy anywhere that she had worked. While she was more passionate about working at Asheville Meadows, she hadn't disliked the grocery store. She couldn't imagine being unhappy as long as she was able to work toward her dreams.

Letting herself back in the house, she unclipped Frankie's leash and gave the dog a couple of treats before leaving again. The drive back to Asheville Meadows was short, and she sat in the car for a couple of minutes before going in, flipping through the healthy cookbook that she had brought along with her. It was almost time to get started on the next month's menu, and she was looking forward to implementing some of the ideas that she had found in the book.

Her phone buzzed just as she was unbuckling her seatbelt. She picked it up and looked at the number, feeling a thrill of excitement when she recognized it as Audrey's phone number.

Was this it? Was Audrey calling to tell her that she either had the job, or had been passed over for someone else? Taking a deep breath, she answered it.

"Hello?"

"Hi, Autumn. I'm glad I caught you. Do you have a couple of minutes to chat?"

"I've got a few," Autumn said. She checked the car's clock. She didn't have to start making lunch for another fifteen minutes.

"Well, I just wanted to let you know that we are beginning to pick up the pieces after what happened here. The restaurant is going to reopen soon, and we still need another chef. What do you say, do you want the position?"

Autumn bit her lip and thought for a second before answering. "Can I give you my answer this evening?" she asked. "I want to talk to my boss here first."

"Of course. Just let us know what you decide. You can call me, and if I don't answer, call the restaurant's landline. Just tell whoever answers that you want to speak with Mrs. Blake."

"I will."

"Let us know either way, okay? You're my first choice, but if you don't want the position, I will offer it to someone else."

"I understand. I'll let you know as soon as I decide."

Autumn hung up and slipped her phone into her purse. Slowly, a grin spread across her face. She had the job, if she wanted it. Her cooking had been good enough. Audrey had liked her. Even if she didn't end up accepting the position, it felt good to know that she had earned it.

Realizing that she had to talk to Nick, her smile dimmed a few notches. Nick had been so supportive of her through all of this. What would he say now that she was actually thinking of leaving?

She was already beginning to doubt herself as she knocked on Nick's office door. When she heard his muted "Come in," she wondered if she should just stay at Asheville Meadows after all. Her uncle's advice had always been sound, and it was true that she did want to work in a restaurant someday, but was now really the best time to upheave her life?

"Are you okay?" Nick asked, glancing up from his desk and frowning. "You look pale. Are you getting sick?"

Autumn took a deep breath. "I got the job," she blurted out.

Multiple emotions flashed across Nick's face too quickly for her to read. Eventually, his expression settled on a look of happiness.

"I knew you would be able to do it," he said. "When do they want you to start?"

"I haven't accepted yet," she said. She stepped into the office and shut the door behind her. "I wanted to talk to you first."

"We've already talked about this," Nick said. "I think you should do it."

"Well, I can't leave here with no notice. And honestly, I love it here and I'm not quite sure I want to go." She hesitated. "I'm thinking of asking Audrey if it would be okay if I agreed to a trial period at the restaurant. Maybe four weeks or so. I could work both places part-time and see if I'm a good fit for such a fast-paced environment. If it doesn't work out, I could just come back here. What do you think?"

"If she will agree to it, I'm perfectly happy to do it," Nick said. "I just want you to make the decision that's best for you."

"I know." She sighed. "I don't know what I want, though. I don't know why this decision is so hard for me to make."

"What did you feel when she told you that you had the job?"

"Happy." Autumn grinned. "Excited. Proud of myself."

"So, what changed? Right now, you look like you've just seen a ghost."

"I don't know. I guess it was the thought of telling you. I would feel bad giving up my position here after only working for a few months. I'll miss seeing you every day, and I will miss working with the people here."

"I don't want you to make this decision based on me or our relationship," Nick said. "Wherever you work, we will still see each other plenty. You can still visit your aunt and uncle, and you will always be welcome to come back here."

"I know. I think that in the long run this could be really good for me, Nick."

"So do I," he said. "So, are you going to do it?"

Autumn took a deep breath. "If she agrees to the trial period, then yes."

CHAPTER ELEVEN

Once the decision was made to accept the job at Blake's Steakhouse, her doubts melted away. This was the job that she had always wanted, and she found herself eager to start.

Her first day would be on Monday, a relatively calm day for the restaurant. That Friday, however, she was supposed to stop in for a couple of hours to pick up her uniform, go over how things worked in the kitchen with Audrey, and sign her contract.

She arranged with the other chef at Asheville Meadows to cover for her on Friday evening, and spent Friday afternoon agonizing over what to wear. She wasn't sure how nicely she should dress. If she was expected to work in the kitchen, she didn't want to be hindered by high heels, but if she was going to be meeting guests, she didn't want to look like she had just woken up, either. She settled on a deep blue button-down blouse, black slacks, and her favorite black flats. She pulled her hair back and kept the makeup to a minimum. Before leaving the house, she paused by the door to run the lint roller over her clothes in case any stray fur from Frankie was sticking to her. The last thing that she wanted was for someone to find a dog hair in their dish.

It was late on Friday evening by the time she got to the restaurant, and the busiest hours were in full swing. She sidled in the door and wound her way around a crowd of people waiting on their reservations, making her way to the hostess in the front.

"I'm here to see Audrey Blake," she said.

"Name?" the distracted hostess asked.

"I'm Autumn Roth."

The young woman snapped to attention and straightened up, self-consciously smoothing her hair. "You're the new chef. It's nice to meet you. Audrey said to go on back to the kitchen. You know the way."

"Thanks."

The restaurant certainly looked different when it was filled with lively customers. She made her way through the building slowly, being careful not to run into any of the hurrying waiters or step on any guests' toes. She was glad that she would be working in the kitchen; she didn't think that she would enjoy spending her hours fighting through the congested dining area to deliver food.

Feeling like an intruder, she pushed through the swinging door to the kitchen and immediately stepped back so as not to be trampled by a hurrying sous chef. She stood with her back against the wall and looked around for Audrey. At last, she spotted the other woman standing next to one of the stoves, arguing with someone over a simmering pan.

Not sure if she should approach or wait until someone noticed her, Autumn tried her best to keep out of the way until Audrey glanced at her direction. Audrey's hand raised in a wave, and Autumn took that is a sign to head over.

"It's a bit crazy right now," Audrey said. "I thought it would be good for you to see what it's like on one of our busiest nights of the week. It won't be this bad on Monday, when you start. You will slowly work up to this."

"Good," Autumn said. "Because I have no idea what's going on."

The other woman chuckled. "It does look chaotic, doesn't it? It's an organized chaos, though. Everyone knows what they're supposed to be doing and where they're supposed to go. It's like a dance; you might not know everyone else's moves, but as long as you know your own, you'll be okay."

"This is a lot different from the kitchen at Asheville Meadows."

"I'd imagine that it is. Come on, I'll take you on a tour. You've already seen the kitchen. This is where you will be spending most of your time, of course, but we've got a nice little staff area in the back. Come this way, it will be quieter there."

Autumn followed Audrey as she wound her way through the kitchen. Audrey held open the door for her, and Autumn stepped through to a quiet, relatively cool hallway. She breathed a sigh of relief. What had she gotten herself into?

"You've already been in my office – it's right over there. The door on the left is the staff area. Go ahead and take a peek."

Autumn walked to the door that Audrey had indicated and pushed it open. Inside was a pleasant little lounge, with comfortable looking furniture, a small kitchenette area, and a flat screen television.

"Sometimes somebody will have a breakdown, and we send them in here to relax and cool off. When you start working the busier evenings, you'll be able to take a breather in this room if you ever start feeling too stressed. It helps keep everyone sane. If you get here early, you're also welcome to spend time here. This is where everyone puts their coats and their purses, and sometimes a change of clothes. You will sweat while you're working, especially in the summer."

"This is nice," Autumn said.

"I worked in a kitchen much like this one when I was younger, before I bought this restaurant. I know how high stress it can be. I've seen plenty of good chefs quit in a rage over something small, and I don't want that to happen here."

"I always find cooking relaxing," Autumn said. "I can't imagine being stressed out by it."

"Wait until you've been here for a couple of weeks," the other woman said, grinning at her. "Let's head to my office now. I'll give you your hat and apron. Once you've reached the end of your trial period, we'll get you an embroidered set with your name on them. We'll also go over the contract. It's nothing too scary, but there are some recipes that we are going to require you not to share. Basically, what happens in the kitchen, stays in the kitchen."

Autumn followed the other woman into her office and took a seat while Audrey dug through her desk. She pulled out a stack of papers and pushed them across the surface to Autumn.

"Give them a look while I go find the apron and hat for you. If you have any questions, just ask."

With that, Audrey got up and left, leaving Autumn alone in the room to go over the contract that spelled out the terms of her job. She picked up the first page and began reading through it. When she got to the salary, her breath caught. It was much more than she made at Asheville Meadows.

She flipped through the next few pages. By the looks of it, her schedule would be busy. She would be expected to work six days a week and would be working nine hours a day most days. She got one week of paid vacation every year but couldn't take it during the restaurant's busiest times. After two years, it would be increased to two weeks of paid vacation.

Feeling a little bit frightened at the responsibility she was about to take on, Autumn turned to the next page. Her mouth was dry, and she looked around for a pitcher of water. Remembering the sink in the staff room, she set the pages down and stood up, stepping out of the office and going into the other room where she found paper cups in the cabinet. She filled one with water and sipped it, beginning to doubt once more whether she had made the right decision.

She felt a little bit more under control after she finished the water and returned to Audrey's office to continue going through the papers. As she shut the door behind her, a draft of air hit the papers and caused them to flutter off the desk. With a sigh, Autumn walked around to the other side of the desk and began gathering the papers up. One had landed in a small metal trash bin. As she picked it up, a crumpled-up sheet of paper underneath caught her attention. It was handwritten, and she saw Audrey's name on it.

With a glance toward the door, she grabbed the crumpled sheet out of the garbage bin and smoothed it out. What she read made her blood run cold.

Audrey,

I know about the fraud. You know what I want. If you don't hire me within a month, I will send all of the information I have to the IRS, and you will be audited. With what you owe, I would be surprised if you don't lose everything.

– B

CHAPTER TWELVE

Autumn folded the paper up and stuck it in her pocket. She couldn't know for sure who B was, but her mind jumped directly to Beatrice. Had Beatrice found something out about Audrey, then threatened her in order to get a job? Had she gone even further and attempted to frame Audrey for murder? Shaken, Autumn sat back down and reached for her purse, not sure who she was going to call, but knowing that somebody had to learn about this besides her.

She heard footsteps behind her, and quickly put her purse down. It seemed important that Audrey didn't know that she had found the letter. Until she knew more about what was going on, she thought it best that it remained her little secret.

Audrey opened the door, carrying a white apron and a chef's hat. "Here you go. Like I said, you'll get your own once you're done with your trial period."

"Thanks," Autumn said, reaching for the bundle. She set it on the table in front of her and glanced the chef's hat. There was a black B embroidered on the band. "Whose are these?"

"Oh, no one that works here. They're just some extras we had lying around." The hat and apron looked like new, and Autumn wondered about the B. Had Audrey bought these in preparation for Beatrice?

"What do you think of the contract?" the other woman asked, sitting down.

"Um, I didn't quite finish going through it," Autumn said. "Can I have just a couple more minutes?"

"Sure. I'll just answer some emails while you finish reading it, if you don't mind."

"Of course not." Autumn turned to the page that she had been on and tried to start reading again, but she couldn't focus. She had too many unanswered questions. After a moment, she cleared her throat. "Excuse me, Audrey?"

The other woman looked up from her computer. "What is it?"

"Did you know that Leo was allergic to sesame oil?"

"I take it you found out who he really was?" Autumn nodded. "No, I didn't. He actually came with the restaurant when I bought it from its previous owners. It wasn't ever something that we spoke about." Her voice caught. "I wish he had told me."

"Why?" Autumn asked, only partially aware that she was speaking out loud. "It wouldn't have changed anything."

"You're right," Audrey said briskly, giving herself a shake. "Go ahead and get back to that contract. I'm glad you're working here, Autumn. Some of the people who wanted the position..." She wrinkled her nose. "Well, let's just say, I think you are by far the best candidate."

Autumn turned her attention back to the contract but couldn't focus no matter how hard she tried. Something was bothering her. Beatrice had already gotten what she wanted. She had blackmailed her way into a position at the restaurant. She had no reason to want Leo dead, and she had no reason to turn to Autumn with the information about the sesame seed oil if she was really the killer. If she had committed the murder, wouldn't she have wanted to keep quiet about it?

At the time, she had thought the Beatrice was the only possible suspect. She hadn't known about Beatrice and Audrey's history, or the blackmail. Now, however, she was beginning to think that she had made a mistake. One thing was certain; she didn't want to work here. Whether Audrey was the killer or not, she didn't want to be involved with a place marred by both blackmail and murder.

Taking a deep breath, Autumn pushed her chair back and stood up. "I'm sorry," she said. "But I don't think this is going to work." She turned to leave, not waiting for Audrey to answer.

"Autumn, wait," the other woman called out. "Hold on – you dropped something. What's wrong?"

Autumn turned to see Audrey holding a crumpled piece of paper out in front of her. Autumn glanced down and patted her pocket. The note must have fallen out of it. It only took Audrey a second to realize what she was holding. "What is this? Were you going through my trash?"

"The papers fell off the desk," Autumn said. "I didn't mean to –"

"Is this why you're leaving?" Audrey asked, angry. "Beatrice is gone now. She's going to jail. You don't have to worry about her anymore."

"It's not –" Autumn broke off. It's not her that I'm worried about, she thought. Audrey froze, seeming to know what Autumn had been about to say even though she had caught herself in time.

"I think you should stay," Audrey said, her voice suddenly cold. "I'll raise the salary. We do require a certain level of... discretion from our employees of course. I understand wanting extra pay if you're expected to keep secrets."

"Keep secrets?" Autumn spluttered, unable to help herself even though she knew that she was in a dangerous situation. "If you expect me to go anywhere other than directly to the police –"

"You are not going to the police," Audrey said in a low, dangerous voice. She strode across the room and grabbed Autumn's wrist, letting the crumpled note fall to the floor. "Blackmail is illegal. Whatever you know, or whatever you think you know, I hope you remember what happened to the last person who tried to blackmail me. She is sitting in a prison cell right now."

"I'm not blackmailing you," Autumn said. "I just want to leave."

"And what are you going to do when you leave?" Audrey said. "What are you going to tell the police?"

"The truth," Autumn said. "That you were being blackmailed, isn't that something that the police should know anyway?"

"The police know as much as they need to know," Audrey said.

The look in the other woman's eyes convinced Autumn that Beatrice had been the target all along. Audrey's grief when Leo died must have been real – she had never meant it to hurt him. She had been aiming for Beatrice. There would have been no way for the police to prove that she knew about Beatrice's allergy. They would have simply assumed that it was an accident. With Beatrice out of the way, Audrey would have been free of the person who was blackmailing her and would have been able to run her restaurant as she liked.

"Let go of me," Autumn snapped, attempting to yank her wrist away, but Audrey's grip was surprisingly strong.

"Not until we reach an understanding," Audrey said, twisting her arm painfully to the side. "I don't know what you know – or what you think you know, but I want to feel confident that you aren't going to open your trap the second you walk out these doors."

"Now who's blackmailing who?" Autumn snapped, the pain in her arm wearing down any good sense that she might have had.

Audrey gave her a tight smile. "This isn't blackmail, dear. This is a threat." Without warning, Audrey's other fist drove into Autumn's stomach. Autumn doubled over, gasping. It took her a long moment to catch her breath again, and by the time she managed it, Audrey had taken her purse from her. Autumn looked up, feeling helpless. Her purse had both her phone and her keys inside it. Now she had no way to call for help, and no way to escape.

"Why did you try to kill her?" Autumn managed. "Why not go to the police? What she was doing was illegal."

"So is evading taxes for half your life," Audrey said. "She might get a slap on the wrist if I went to the police with the information about her blackmailing me, but I would end up in federal prison. There's no way I could ever pay the fines that I owe for all of my back taxes. I knew when she sent me this note that this wouldn't be the end of it. She would get a job here, then she would start asking for more and more, and it would never let up. I wasn't about to let someone control my life like that. I didn't even come up with the plan to kill her until she let slip about her allergy while we were in my office. A little flick of my wrist, and your mashed cauliflower had a new ingredient added in. I figured it wouldn't hurt anyone else, but it would kill her. Before leaving the kitchen, I had Kiki get the plates out, which gave me enough time to add the oil without her seeing. I wasn't expecting Leo to have a reaction to it. He was a great chef, and a good friend. That's the only thing in all of this I'm sorry about. Well, that, and the fact that it didn't work."

"You are insane," Autumn said.

"She was going to suck me dry," Audrey said, her voice rising. "How could I live my life with someone like her draining my resources every time she wanted something else? Where would it end? How much money would she end up asking for? Would she demand the whole restaurant one day? No, this was the only way out. What she was doing was illegal too, and I wouldn't have felt bad about killing a criminal."

I need my phone, Autumn thought, staring at the purse. *Or my keys. Anything. There is no way I can get help without* – She froze, feeling stupid. She was in a restaurant full of people. She was standing with her back to the door, and Audrey was a few feet away from her. She had regained her breath enough that she was no longer gasping for air. If only she had the courage, she could make a run for it, and help would be only a few steps away.

"After all of this, am I supposed to think that you wouldn't try the same thing with me?" Autumn asked. "Even if I agreed to let you pay me off so I wouldn't go to the police, I already know that you will kill someone who blackmails you. How would this be any different than living with Beatrice over your shoulder?"

To her surprise, Audrey actually seemed to think about that for a moment. The other woman frowned. "You're just making this worse for yourself, aren't you?"

She seemed to make up her mind about something after a moment. Walking backward, never taking her eyes off of Autumn, she made her way to the other side of the desk and pulled open a drawer. Not sure what the woman was looking for – was she about to pull out a gun? A knife? – Autumn reached for the doorknob behind her. She turned the handle slowly, then yanked the door open and slipped into the hall. She heard Audrey's enraged shout behind her but didn't stop to look back. She ran toward the door that led to the kitchen and burst through, nearly knocking a waiter off of his feet. She wanted to stop and ask for help then and there, but she didn't know if she could trust the kitchen staff. Just how devoted were they to their boss? Instead, she shoved her way through the kitchen and out into the dining area, where she skidded to a stop at the first table she saw.

"Call the police," she gasped. "Someone's trying to kill me."

EPILOGUE

"I have to say, I'm glad you came back," Nick said. He was leaning against the counter while Autumn chopped up a bell pepper.

"So am I," Autumn said. "Though I can't say the circumstances were the best."

"Yes, I could have done without you facing off against a murderess." He sighed and ran his hands through his hair, looking tired. "Has anyone ever told you that you are a very stressful person to date sometimes?"

"Sorry," Autumn said. "I promise it's not every day that I almost get myself killed."

"It sure seems like it is," he said. "I'm glad you're all right. And I really am glad that you're back. This place wouldn't have been the same without you."

"I was having doubts about my decision even before I realized that Audrey was the killer," Autumn said. "I think I would have come back here anyway. I love this place. I wouldn't have ever felt at home there."

"I'm glad to know that you didn't make this decision just because someone held a gun to your face," he said.

"Actually, she didn't have a gun," Autumn said, "When I gave my statement to the officer who arrested her, he told me that she had been looking for a pen. She told him when she confessed that she was going to have me sign a statement that I was the one who had killed Leo. That way if I ever tried to blackmail her with my knowledge, she would have been able to control me with that."

"That's actually a pretty good solution," Nick said, sounding surprised. "It does make my mind rest easier to know that you weren't about to be shot or stabbed."

"Mine too," Autumn said. "I feel terrible about what I did to Beatrice, though. She might not have been exactly innocent, but she didn't deserve to go to jail for a crime she didn't commit. Once she gets released and everything is straightened out, she's going to hate me."

"Maybe not. She was probably safer there than she would have been out in the world with Audrey on her tail. I doubt Audrey would have left it at only one attempt to kill her."

"You might be right," Autumn said. "Either way, I think I'm going to watch my back from here on out."

"That's no way to live," Nick said. "We will all watch out for you here. Like you said, you're like family. Your aunt and uncle and I aren't the only ones who would've missed you. I know Emily would have been crushed if you left. That young woman looks up to you."

"Well, I'm not going anywhere," Autumn said. "I've learned my lesson. I think I am happier here than I ever would be in a five-star restaurant. Sometimes dreams do change, and I guess it just took me a while to realize that."

Printed in Great Britain
by Amazon